ANGEL PARADE PILE UP

Created & Written by MISTY TAGGART
Illustrated by KAREN BELL

with Angel Heaven Love — Misty

WORD PUBLISHING
Dallas • London • Vancouver • Melbourne

Behind the third cloud to the right,
just around the corner from the rainbow, is The Angel Academy.
This is where young angels learn to be real guardian angels.

Managing Editor: Laura Minchew *Project Editor:* Beverly Phillips

Library of Congress Cataloging-in-Publication Data

Taggart, Misty, 1940–
Angel parade pileup/created and written by Misty Taggart;
illustrated by Karen Bell.
p. cm. (The angel academy; #1)
"Word kids!"
Summary: Unhappy because she is too young to build her own float for the Annual Angel Parade, Mirth and her pet cloud Puffaluff sabotage the other angels' creations.
ISBN 0-8499-5016-3
[1. Guardian angels—Fiction. 2. Angels—Fiction. 3. Behavior—Fiction. 4. Parades—Fiction.] I. Bell, Karen, 1949– ill. II. Title
III. Series: Taggart, Misty, 1940– Angel academy; #1.
PZ7.T1284Ap 1994
[E]—dc20

94-25673
CIP
AC

Printed in the United States of America 94 95 96 97 98 99 LBM 9 8 7 6 5 4 3 2 1

STARIA

She thinks she's very grown-up, but don't you believe it.

ASTRID

Her laugh is as big as her sweet tooth.

JUBILATE

He's ready to right every wrong—and has a lot of fun doing it.

ANGELUS

If you have a question about anything, he has the answer—he thinks.

MIRTH

She may be small, but she can be big trouble.

The guardian angels-in-training were very excited. Tomorrow's big parade had them forgetting about their studies. "Your holiday doesn't start until tomorrow. Today's classes aren't over yet," reminded Miss Celestial.

"Yep, they are!" announced George the Heavenly Handyman, as he entered the classroom. "Your chalkboard's missing a screw. I'm here to fix it."

Staria whispered to Astrid, "See, it worked! We're getting out early!"

Astrid proudly held the missing screw she had removed. "Yeah, pretty sneaky idea, Staria."

Then suddenly, "Oops!" The screw fell from Astrid's hand and onto the floor. It rolled right up to the front of the class. "Uh-oh!" Astrid slid down in her seat.

George smiled. "Well, what do you know? Just the screw I needed."

"Astrid will stay after class and clean erasers," said Miss Celestial. "But everyone else is excused."

The others cheered and headed for the door.

"Good-bye, Miss Celestial," Staria called, as she left the room. "Too bad, Astrid."

George couldn't help but feel sorry for Astrid. "You know better than to listen to Staria. That cherub loves to get you in trouble."

"I know. But I just wanted to get started on my parade float early." Chalk dust flew as Astrid banged erasers together. She was mad at herself for letting Staria talk her into doing something she knew was wrong.

The next day, before the Annual Angel Parade and Picnic, most of the angels were putting the final touches on their floats. "Hey, Mirth, bring me those pink and purple starglazer flowers," called Staria.

"I'd rather be in school than have to work on everyone else's floats," mumbled Mirth.

Mirth was the littlest angel-in-training. She and her pet cloud Puffaluff were not having a good day. "I'm five and a half!" she had pleaded. But she was just too little to build a float by herself. To make matters worse, all of her friends kept asking her to help them—*"Mirth, please do this; Mirth, bring me that; Mirth, get out of the way. . . ."*

"I hope none of them win the Best Float Trophy!" the little angel complained to Puffaluff.

Meanwhile, Astrid and Jubilate were admiring the huge trophy and arguing over whose float was the best. Astrid boasted, "No one's ever built an astroswirl float—it will be delicious!" (Astroswirl is like ice cream, only better.)

"I made a giant skateboard. And it's cool," said Jubilate. "The trophy's mine for sure!"

"Oh, dear! My little angels have a lot to learn about sharing and being thoughtful of others," said their teacher, Miss Celestial.

Stella the Starduster had been shining the Best Float Trophy all day. Her job was to keep Angel Heaven squeaky clean.

"Step back, cherubs! I don't want to see any fingerprints on this trophy," she warned.

"Look at that hat," Staria giggled, whispering to Astrid. "Isn't it the funniest thing ever?"

It had bows and feathers and whatnots and whatchamacallits sticking out in every direction. Stella owned a zillion hats of all shapes and colors, but this one was her favorite. Staria liked hats, too. But not silly hats like Stella's!

Meanwhile, Puffaluff had been trying to cheer up Mirth by making funny cloud shapes. That always made her giggle, but not today. So Puffaluff thought of doing something funny and naughty—even a little mean.

First, Puffaluff flew over the shiny trophy. The sunny day became very foggy.

"Get out of here, you bag of wind!" cried Stella. And she swooshed Puffaluff away with one of her brooms. That just made Puffaluff mad . . . so what did he do? He rained on the trophy, of course.

It was almost time for the parade to begin. Stella quickly cleaned the trophy again. And all the angels hurried off to put the final touches on their floats.

Jubilate brushed the last coat of bright red paint on his giant skateboard.

Astrid added another dollop of whipped cream to her gigantic Astroswirl Banana Split Supreme.

Angelus, the very smart angel, had made a huge float with all sorts of wheels and belts and gears and whistles. None of the other angels knew exactly what it was supposed to be, but it looked and sounded very important.

"It's a mechanical masterpiece!" Angelus declared proudly.

Now each angel in Angel Heaven is given a very special talent. Staria's talent was that she could make flowers bloom by just speaking to them. Her float was a beautiful garden with blooming flowers of all kinds.

Staria was busy talking to her flowers. She didn't see Puffaluff and Mirth sneak up behind her float. Puffaluff motioned for Mirth to pick up some clippers.

"I don't know, Puff," said Mirth. "It really wouldn't be very nice to ruin Staria's float. But, she's been so bossy, making me help her while she takes all the credit." Puffaluff grinned as Mirth moved toward the flowers with the clippers.

Next, with Mirth as the lookout, Puffaluff quickly loosened a screw on Jubilate's huge skateboard float.

Then Puffaluff and Mirth made a hole in the bottom of the *gigantic* banana-split dish.

The naughty cloud also decided that Angelus's float needed a little rewiring.

A great cheer went up as the Angel Band began to play. The horns, harps, and hand bells were all making a heavenly sound. It was time for the parade to begin.

"This is going to be so funny," giggled Mirth as she thought about the pranks they had played on their friends. Puffaluff grinned in agreement.

But Staria didn't think it was a bit funny. "What happened to all my beautiful flowers?" Her float was ruined. And there was no time to fix it. "Who could have done such a terrible thing?" Tears filled her eyes as the other floats started down the street.

Astrid's banana-split float was first. And as Puffaluff had planned, it began to melt. The astroswirl oozed through the hole onto the street in front of the judges' platform.

Puffaluff was enjoying his joke. But Mirth looked a little worried. "Isn't that melted astroswirl going to be slippery?"

Jubilate's float rolled toward the judges. *The trophy's almost mine!* he thought, smiling and waving to Miss Celestial and the crowd.

Then it happened! His float hit the melted astroswirl and went into a skid! A surprised Jubilate tried to get his skateboard under control. But the wheel Puffaluff had loosened popped off!

"Yikes!" yelled Jubilate. Then—*CRASH!* His float collided with Astrid's melted banana split!

Next came Angelus on his mechanical masterpiece. He was having trouble, too. His float was making the most unheavenly noises.

CLANK! CLUNK! SPUTTER! COUGH!

"Look out!" Angelus yelled, jumping off the float just as wheels, belts, and bolts exploded into the air! Everyone ran for cover.

"Oh, Puff, look what happened to my friends!" Mirth cried. "We've ruined the parade! Why did I let you talk me into this?"

After the parade, all the angels and angels-in-training went to Cumulus Park for the picnic. Everyone, but Mirth, was having lots of fun. After all, angels don't stay mad for long.

"It looks like no one will be getting the trophy this year," Miss Celestial said. She offered Mirth a big slice of angel food cake.

"I'm sorry I ruined the parade and my friends' floats," said Mirth. "I knew it was wrong." Big tears ran down the little angel's cheeks.

"Mirth, you must be careful not to let others talk you into doing things you know you shouldn't do," said Miss Celestial.

"Puff just wanted me to have fun. But now, I'm in trouble and he's not," complained Mirth.

"Oh, I wouldn't say that. Take a look over there." Miss Celestial smiled as she pointed to a crowd gathered around one of the games.

A group of angels cheered as Jubilate grabbed a ball. "This is gonna be fun!" He took a big windup and pitched hard. The ball hit the bull's-eye.

The seat collapsed, and an annoyed Puffaluff dropped into the water. *KERSPLASH!*

"My turn!" yelled Astrid, picking up another ball.

Everyone soon forgot the float pileup. And Mirth felt loved and accepted again. She had learned an important lesson.

As for the trophy . . . well, each one of Miss Celestial's guardian angels-in-training was certain that he or she would win it next year . . . even Mirth.